To my family and Stacey

—M.G.

To my mother and my father

—B.N.

Text copyright © 1999 by Mike Gibbie

Illustrations copyright © 1999 by Barbara Nascimbeni

All rights reserved.

CIP Data is available.

Published in the United States 2000 by Dutton Children's Books,

a division of Penguin Putnam Books for Young Readers

345 Hudson Street, New York, New York 10014

http://www.penguinputnam.com

Originally published in Great Britain 1999 by Macmillan Children's Books, London

Printed in Belgium   First American Edition

2 4 6 8 10 9 7 5 3 1

ISBN 0-525-46397-6

MIKE GIBBIE • illustrated by **BARBARA NASCIMBENI**

Small Brown Dog's Bad Remembering Day

Dutton Children's Books • **New York**

Small Brown Dog was having a really bad remembering day.

He couldn't remember which side to get out of bed.
He couldn't remember what he liked for breakfast.

Worst of all, he couldn't remember his name!

"If only I could find my collar, that would tell me my name," he said.

But he couldn't remember where he had left it. He looked high and low. But he couldn't find it anywhere in his doghouse.

So he ran outside...

...and very nearly ran into Tess the Terrier delivering the mail.

"Help, Tess! I've lost my collar, and I don't know **WHO I AM!**"

"You," said Tess, "are a small brown dog
with a pink nose,
but I don't remember your name."

"Can't you remember anything else?"
asked Small Brown Dog.

Tess thought hard. "You like splashing in puddles."

"You're right!" said
Small Brown Dog,
and he set off to find some.

He was
splashing
down the street
when he saw
Dan the Dalmatian.
"Help, Dan! I've lost my collar,
and I don't know **WHO I AM!**"

"You," said Dan, "are a small brown dog
with a pink nose
who likes splashing in puddles,
but I don't remember your name."

"Can't you remember anything else?"
asked Small Brown Dog.
Dan thought hard. "You're always chasing squirrels."
"You're right!" said Small Brown Dog,
and he set off for the park.

At the park he ran into
Bobby the Bulldog.
   "Help, Bobby! I've lost my collar,
and I don't know **WHO I AM!**"

   "You," said Bobby, "are a small brown dog
with a pink nose
who likes splashing in puddles
and is always chasing squirrels,
but I don't remember
your name."

"Can't you remember anything else?"
asked Small Brown Dog.
Bobby thought hard. "You've got a bad case of fleas."
"You're right!" said Small Brown Dog,
and he hurried off, scratching.

He went across the road and into the hairdresser's,
where he saw Peaches the Poodle.

"Help, Peaches! I've lost my collar,
and I don't know **WHO I AM!**"

"You," said Peaches,
"are a small brown dog
with a pink nose
who likes splashing in puddles,
is always chasing squirrels, and
has a bad case of fleas,
but I don't remember your name."

"Can't you remember
anything else?" asked Small Brown Dog.
    Peaches thought hard. "You can't resist hot dogs."
    "You're right!" said Small Brown Dog,
and he remembered that he was hungry.

He turned the corner into the square,
where he saw **Sid the Sausage Dog.**
  "Help, Sid! I've lost my collar, and I don't know **WHO I AM!**"
  "You," said Sid, "are a small brown dog with a pink nose
who likes splashing in puddles, is always chasing squirrels,
has a bad case of fleas, and can't resist hot dogs,
but I don't remember your name."

"Can't you remember anything else?"
asked Small Brown Dog.
   Sid thought hard. "You bury bones in the sand."
   "You're right!" said Small Brown Dog,
and he set off to dig one up.

He went across the square
and into the building site,
where he saw Ralph the Rottweiler.
"Help, Ralph! I've lost my collar,
and I don't know WHO I AM!"

"You," said Ralph,
"are a small brown dog
with a pink nose
who likes splashing in puddles,
is always chasing squirrels,
has a bad case of fleas,
can't resist hot dogs, and
buries bones in the sand,
but I don't remember your name."

"Can't you remember anything else?"
asked Small Brown Dog.
Ralph thought hard. "You blow a big shiny trumpet."
"You're right!" said Small Brown Dog,
and he set off to join his band.

He went over the hill and into the park,
where he saw Charlie the Chihuahua.
   "Help, Charlie! I've lost my collar,
and I don't know WHO I AM!"

   "You," said Charlie,
"are a small brown dog
with a pink nose
who likes splashing in puddles,
is always chasing squirrels,
has a bad case of fleas,
can't resist hot dogs,
buries bones in the sand, and
blows a big shiny trumpet,
but I don't remember your name."

"Can't you remember
anything else?"
asked Small Brown Dog.
Charlie thought hard.
"You're always losing your collar."
"I know that!" said Small Brown Dog.
"But where can I find it?"
"You could try the police station," said Charlie.
"You're right!" said Small Brown Dog,
and he set off to do just that.

He ran back through the park, across the road,
up the street, and into the police station,
where Alf the Alsatian was standing behind the desk.
   "Help, Alf! I've lost my collar and—"

   "Here it is!" said Alf. "Roger the Retriever
brought it in this morning."
   "At last I remember," said Small Brown Dog.

"I'm a small brown dog
with a pink nose

who likes splashing in puddles,

is always chasing squirrels,

has a bad case of fleas,

can't resist hot dogs,

buries bones in the sand,

blows a big shiny trumpet,

and is always losing his collar,
and my name is..."

"But I could have told you that!"